This edition contains the following copyrighted works:

Hugs and Kisses © 2001 by NordSüd Verlag AG, CH 8005 Zürich, Switzerland.
First published in Switzerland under the title *Mama, ich hab dich lieb*.
English translation © 2001 by North-South Books Inc., New York 10001.

Don't Worry, Wags © 2003 by NordSüd Verlag AG, CH 8005 Zürich, Switzerland.
First published in Switzerland under the title *Mama, wo bist du?*
English translation © 2003 by North-South Books Inc., New York 10001.

Wiggles © 2004 by NordSüd Verlag AG, CH 8005 Zürich, Switzerland.
First published in Switzerland under the title *Papa, was ist das?*
English translation © 2005 by North-South Books Inc., New York 10001.

Compilation first published in the United States, Great Britain, Canada, Australia, and
New Zealand in 2010 by North-South Books Inc., an imprint of NordSüd Verlag AG,
CH-8005 Zürich, Switzerland.
Distributed in the United States by North-South Books Inc., New York 10001.

Library of Congress Cataloging-in-Publication Data is available.
ISBN: 978-0-7358-2294-8 (trade edition)
Printed in China by Toppan Leefung Packaging & Printing (Dongguan) Co., Ltd.,
Dongguan, P.R.C., January 2010.
1 3 5 7 9 ❖ 10 8 6 4 2

www.northsouth.com

Christophe Loupy · Eve Tharlet

PUPPY LOVE
A LITTER OF PUPPY STORIES

INCLUDES

HUGS and KISSES
DON'T WORRY, WAGS
WIGGLES

NorthSouth
New York / London

HUGS
and
Kisses

One morning Hugs the puppy woke up early. His mother and father and all his sisters were still sleeping. Quietly he tiptoed outside. There was something he had to find out.

"Good morning," called two ducks from the pond. "What are you doing up so early?"

"I'm finding out something," Hugs said. "Could you please give me a kiss?"

"A kiss?" quacked the ducks. "Of course. Where would you like it?"

"Right here," said Hugs, and he pointed to his cheek.

So the ducks came out of the water and each gave him a kiss: one on the left and one on the right.

Hugs closed his eyes and smiled. He'd never ever had a kiss from a duck! It was a bit hard of course, and wet, but it was quite refreshing.

Hugs thanked the ducks and went on.

Out in the pasture Hugs saw a horse. "Good morning!" he called.

"Good morning," answered the horse. "It's nice of you to visit."

"I was wondering," Hugs said shyly. "Could you please give me a kiss?"

"A kiss?" neighed the horse.

"Yes. Right here." Hugs pointed to his forehead.

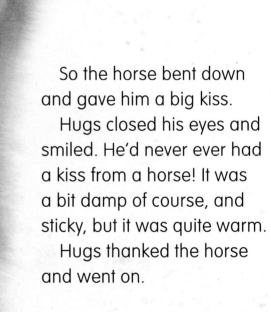

So the horse bent down and gave him a big kiss.

Hugs closed his eyes and smiled. He'd never ever had a kiss from a horse! It was a bit damp of course, and sticky, but it was quite warm.

Hugs thanked the horse and went on.

Soon the puppy found a pig rolling in a puddle of mud.

"Good morning," said Hugs.

"Good morning to you," answered the pig. "What are you doing here all alone?"

"I'm finding out something," Hugs said. "Could you please give me a kiss?"

"A kiss from me?" grunted the pig.

"Yes. Right here." Hugs pointed to the tip of his nose.

So the pig stepped out of the mud and gave him a kiss right on the tip of his nose.

Hugs closed his eyes and smiled. He'd never ever had a kiss from a pig! It was a bit muddy of course, and the bristles scratched a little, but it was quite tender.

Hugs thanked the pig and went on.

Hugs came to a garden fence. There he spied a rabbit out among the corn.

"Good morning," he called.

"What are you doing so far from home?" asked the rabbit.

"I'm finding out something," Hugs said. "Could you please give me a kiss?"

"A kiss from me?" murmured the rabbit.

"Yes. Right here." Hugs pointed to his neck.

The rabbit hopped closer and gave him a kiss right in his wrinkled fur.

Hugs closed his eyes and smiled. He'd never ever had a kiss from a rabbit! It was a bit wiggly of course, and quick, but it was quite soft.

Hugs thanked the rabbit and headed back home.

On the way, Hugs saw a yellow butterfly. "Good morning," he called.

"Morning, morning!" whispered the butterfly in the wind. "You have been out for a long time!"

"I'm heading home," Hugs said. "But first, could you give me a kiss?"

"A kiss from me?" The butterfly dipped his wings.

"Yes, please. A kiss right here." Hugs pointed to his mouth.

So the butterfly settled gently on his mouth and gave him a kiss.

Hugs closed his eyes again and smiled. Oh, so fine, a butterfly's kiss! He'd never felt anything like it before. It tickled a bit of course, but it was wonderful.

Hugs thanked the butterfly with all his heart and hurried on home.

His mother and father and sisters were all waiting for him.

"Where have you been?" asked Mother. "We were worried about you."

"Oh, it was such a beautiful morning, I couldn't sleep. And there was something I had to find out."

"Now, my little one, what was so important?" Mother nuzzled Hugs and gave him a big kiss.

"That's it!" Hugs said. "Now I know.
A kiss from a duck is refreshing.
A kiss from a horse is warm.
A kiss from a pig is tender.
A kiss from a rabbit is soft.
A kiss from a butterfly is wonderful . . .
But the best kiss of all is the kiss I get from you!"

DON'T WORRY, WAGS

Wags was a worrier. When her brother and sisters played hide-and-seek in the haystack, Wags worried that she'd be trapped beneath all that hay. When the other puppies scampered into the farmyard, Wags worried about unexpected dangers. When the other puppies splashed happily in a big puddle, Wags worried that she might fall in and drown. Yes, Wags was a worrier.

One morning, Mother called, "Hop up! We're going to the farmers' market!"

Wags watched her brother and sisters bound into the truck.

"Are you sure it's safe up there?" she asked.

"It's perfectly safe," said Mother. "Don't worry, Wags!"

The engine rumbled and the truck bounced along.

Wags shivered with fear. "How far is it?" she asked nervously. "What is a farmers' market? Is it dangerous?"

Mother laughed. "Don't worry, Wags," she said. "The market is fun. And it's not dangerous if you stay right with me."

The market was incredible—so big and bright and busy. Wags followed along behind her family.

Suddenly Wags stopped. She stuck her nose in the air. Ooh! Aah! The smells! Wags looked around and saw a mountain of sausages. She saw a giant ham. Everything smelled delicious.

Then she saw the butcher with his knife. She hurried to catch up to her family.

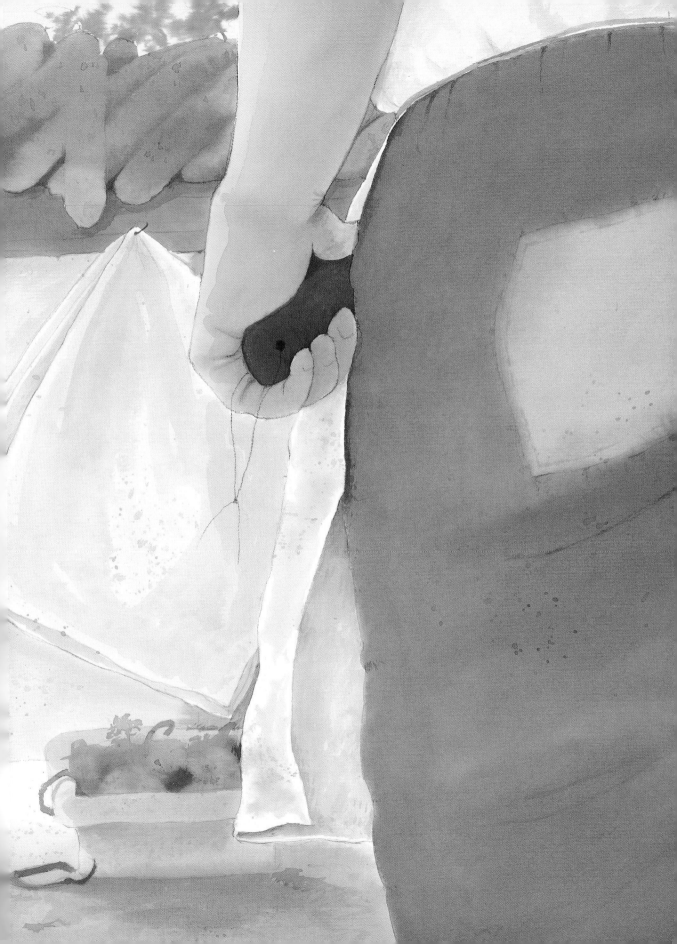

But where *were* they? Wags looked left and right. All she could see were legs—hundreds of legs walking this way and that. Dangerous legs that could step on a little puppy.

Wags cried out, "Mother! Father! Where are you? **Arf! Arf! Arooouuu!**"

But nobody answered.

All alone, Wags wandered around looking for her family. She saw a nanny goat with her baby kid. Wags wanted to be with *her* mother. She started to cry.

"Who are you, and why are you crying?" asked the nanny goat.

"I'm Wags, and I lost my mother," said Wags, sniffling.

"Don't worry, Wags. She can't be far," said the goat. "And she is surely looking for you. Why don't you climb up on something tall so you can get a better view?"

Wags saw a big stone fountain. It was tall.
She scrambled up over the edge. **SPLASH!**
Wags landed headfirst in the water. She
sputtered and climbed out, shaking herself
dry. What a dangerous fountain, she thought.

Meow! A scruffy cat jumped gracefully onto the edge of the fountain. "Who are you? Are you looking for fish?" he asked.

"I'm Wags, and I'm looking for my family," Wags whimpered.

"Don't worry, Wags. Maybe I can help. Where did you see them last?"

"Near the sausages," said Wags.

"That must be the butcher's stall," said the cat. "Follow me. I know just where it is."

The sausages were there. The ham was there. The butcher was there. But Wags's family was not there. Wags trembled forlornly.

"Don't worry, Wags," said the cat. "Wait here while I look for a policeman to help."

Wags sighed and sat down to wait.

A string of sausages dangled over her head. The smell made her tummy growl. Cautiously, Wags licked one. It was oh so delicious! She took just a nibble. Mmmm. She took a bite. Before she knew it, the string of sausages slipped off the table. The butcher began to shout.

Terrified, Wags ran for her life.

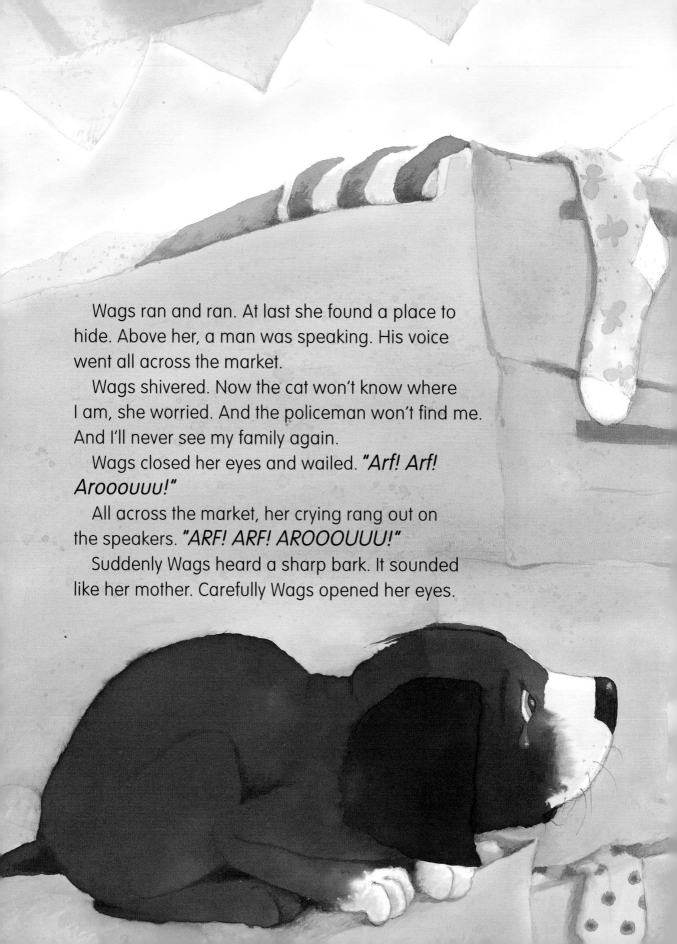

Wags ran and ran. At last she found a place to hide. Above her, a man was speaking. His voice went all across the market.

Wags shivered. Now the cat won't know where I am, she worried. And the policeman won't find me. And I'll never see my family again.

Wags closed her eyes and wailed. *"Arf! Arf! Arooouuu!"*

All across the market, her crying rang out on the speakers. *"ARF! ARF! AROOOUUU!"*

Suddenly Wags heard a sharp bark. It sounded like her mother. Carefully Wags opened her eyes.

It *was* her mother—and her father and her brother and her sisters too!

"Don't worry, Wags," said Mother, kissing her softly on the head. "We're here now."

"We looked everywhere for you," said Father. "And then we heard you calling."

Wags stayed right between her parents for the rest of the day. The market was fun and not at all dangerous. They found the cat and thanked him. Later they found a long string of delicious sausages that had been thrown away behind the butcher's stall.

When it was time to go home, Wags was the first one on the truck. "Can I go again next time?" she asked.

"Don't worry, Wags," said Mother. "We'll never go anywhere without you!"

WIGGLES

"**C**ock-a-doodle-doo!"

As soon as the rooster crowed one morning, Father quietly got up.

Wiggles was wide awake too. "Where are you going?" she asked.

"Shhh!" whispered Father. "Don't wake the others. I'm going for a walk. Come with me."

In the yard, the farmer's wife was already at work.
"Where is she going?" asked Wiggles.
"Wait and see, Wiggles," Father replied.

In the barn, the farmer's wife began to milk the cow.

"What is she doing?" asked Wiggles.

"Wait!" said Father.

But Wiggles was too curious to wait. She moved closer, and a few drops of milk landed on her tongue.

"Yumm! That's good!" said Wiggles.

Suddenly there was a loud buzzing noise outside.
"What is *that*?" asked Wiggles.
"Let's go outside and see," said Father.
But Wiggles saw a quicker way. She scampered up the coal pile and looked out of the window. A red helicopter flew right over the farm, making a terrible racket.

Startled, Wiggles tumbled down the coal pile and knocked over the bucket of milk. Now she was covered in soot and milk. Father laughed. "Just look at you, Wiggles!" he said.

Wiggles and Father headed out to the farmyard. They saw the farmer's wife carrying a basket.

"Where is she going now?" asked Wiggles.

"Wait and see," Father replied.

Wiggles followed, wiggling with excitement.

When they reached the chicken coop, Wiggles watched
the farmer's wife collect eggs.

Wiggles went to investigate. She pushed her nose right
into a nest.

"Watch out!" warned Father.

Too late! Wiggles fell into the nest, breaking the eggs.

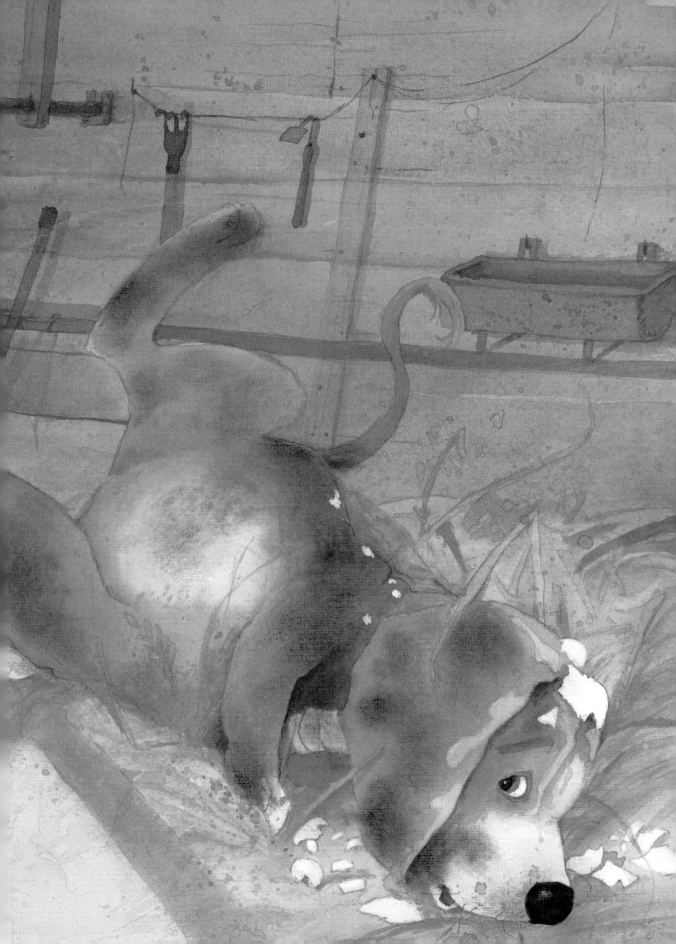

"Eggs are good too!" said Wiggles, happily licking the egg off her face.

Father gave her a lick. "Yes, they're delicious!" he said. "And so are you!"

Just then the farmer's wife headed out to the orchard.

"Where is she going?" asked Wiggles.

"Let's see," Father replied.

They followed the farmer's wife to the orchard.
"Those houses are pretty!" exclaimed Wiggles.
"Don't go near them!" warned Father. "They're
beehives, and bees don't like to be disturbed."
"I'm just going to say hello," said Wiggles.

Wiggles poked her nose into one of the hives.
When she pulled it back out, it was covered with honey.
"Mmm! That smells good!" said Wiggles.

The bees buzzed angrily all around her.
"Help!" cried Wiggles, and she ran away as fast as she could.

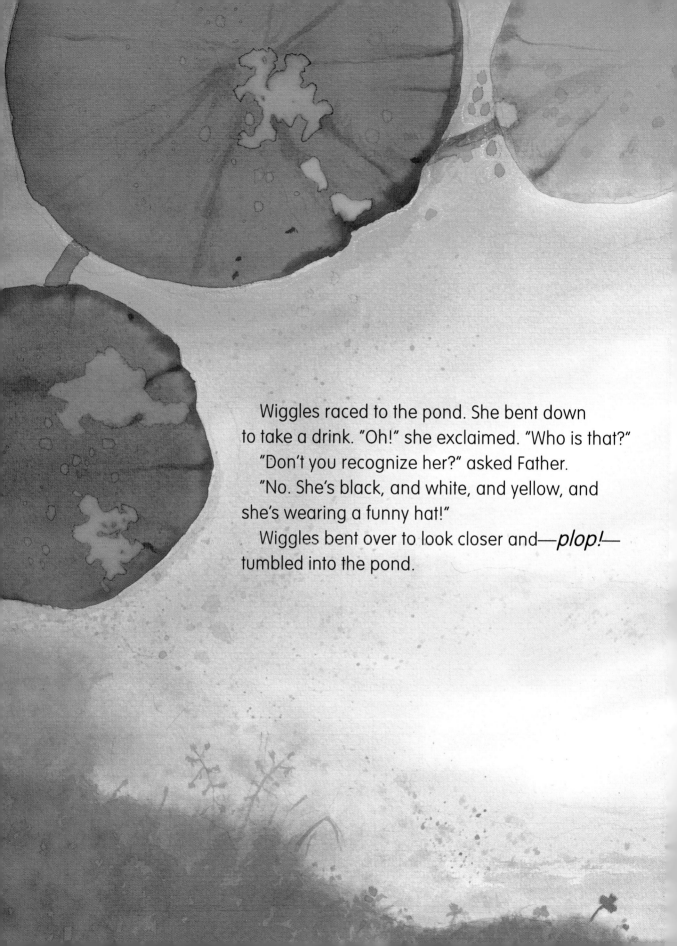

Wiggles raced to the pond. She bent down to take a drink. "Oh!" she exclaimed. "Who is that?"

"Don't you recognize her?" asked Father.

"No. She's black, and white, and yellow, and she's wearing a funny hat!"

Wiggles bent over to look closer and—*plop!*—tumbled into the pond.

"Ha!" exclaimed Father. "Well, you really needed a bath."

"Look! I can swim!" Wiggles said proudly.

Father jumped in too. Then he and Wiggles played hide-and-seek among the water lilies.

When they got back to the farm, Mother and the other puppies were just waking up.

Wiggles snuggled against her mother. "I had milk and eggs and honey, and I went swimming too," she told her.

"What a nice dream you had!" said Mother, giving Wiggles a soft kiss. "But what are you going to do now that it's time to get up?"

"Wait and see . . . ," said Wiggles, yawning. And she fell fast asleep.